Rising Stars

Written by Renu Mehta

Illustrated by Suman S. Roy

Starlight

For the Parent / Teacher

'Must Know' words are common words that are found in everyday print. These words are used often and are non-decodable (impossible to sound out). Hence, it is essential that children develop automatic recognition of these words to enhance their reading fluency, comprehension and confidence. As such, they constitute an important step towards the child's reading ability.

- Find quiet time to read with the child regularly. Remember practise makes perfect.
- Make sure that the child looks and points at the first letter of the words to facilitate reading. After reading each page, encourage the child to re-read the 'Must Know' words at the bottom of the page.
- DO NOT move on to the next story until the child recognises all the 'Must Know' words in the story.
- Ask questions about the story and the child's feelings.
- Photocopy and play word bingo.

'Must Know' words used in this book

We are a Family		We are Busy		We are Laughing	
and	the	his	was	for	as
he	is	in	with	that	a
are	on	to	it	of	you

We are a Family

This is my dad. He is working on his computer work pad. Click! Click! Click!

is he on

This is my mum. She is baking chocolate and strawberry cupcakes.

Yum! Yum! Yum!

is and

This is my brother Roneel.

He is hungry. Are there any cheese sandwiches for his meal?

Munch! Munch! Munch!

is are he

This is my brother Nihar. He is eating jam from the jar.

Omm nom nom! Omm nom nom! Omm nom nom!

is he the

This is my dog Milo. He is happy eating the enormous pink marshmallows.

Slobber! Slobber! Slobber!

I am Tara. I am singing and dancing to my favourite song on the radio with my friend Sara.

Lalala! Lalala! Lalala!

and on the

We all are happy. We all are a happy family.

Ahh ha! Ahh ha! Ahh ha!

Starboard

Jobs to do

Play bingo!

Call out a word and let the child place her finger on the corresponding word.

and	on	is	the
he	are	and	on
the	is	he	are

Starboard

Talking point

1. *What is making click, click sounds in dad's office?*
2. *Where is mum?*
3. *What is mum doing?*
4. *What sandwiches does the child like?*
5. *What jam is Nihar eating?*
6. *Ask the child about a pet she would like to keep.*
7. *What is the child's favourite song? Ask her to sing it.*
8. *Explore what makes the child happy.*

We are Busy

it

in

with

his

to

was

Dad was busy working away in his office alone.

Sometimes filing and sometimes on the phone.

Tring! Tring! Tring! Tring! Tring! Tring!

was his in

Mum was busy at home answering all the knocks at the door. Sometimes cooking and sometimes mopping the floor.

Swish swash! Swish swash! Swish swash!

Nihar was busy being naughty in school.

Sometimes it was during the English class and sometimes in the swimming pool.

Splash! Splash! Splash!

was in it

Roneel was busy punching the boys.

Sometimes playing chase with the girls and sometimes fighting over toys.

Ouch! Ouch! Ouch!

was with

Milo was busy in the garden digging holes.

Sometimes chasing the rabbits and sometimes running around looking for moles.

Woof! Woof! Woof!

was in

They all were busy but I was not. I was feeling awfully sick. Waiting for mum's magic pill to do the trick!

Pop-pop! Pop-pop! Pop-pop!

was to

We all are busy. We all are a busy family!

Rush! Rush! Rush!

Starboard

Jobs to do

Play bingo!

Call out a word and let the child place her finger on the corresponding word.

was	with	his	in
to	it	was	with
in	his	to	it

Starboard

Talking point

1. *What is dad doing in his office?*

2. *Who is mopping the floor?*

3. *What is Nihar doing?*

4. *Ask the child about being naughty.*

5. *Was Roneel being a good boy? Why not?*

6. *What was Milo busy with?*

7. *What is wrong with Tara?*

8. *Discuss why being annoying is not nice.*

We are Laughing

When dad dresses up as a clown and makes funny faces to make us laugh.

We know that he is the best dad anyone can have.

Giggle! Giggle! Giggle!

as a that

When mum thinks she is a pop star and sings a song.

Her words are jumbled and her tune is all wrong.

Chickaboom! Chickaboom! Chickaboom!

When Roneel thinks he is a fluffy bunny that can hop.

He destroys mum's veggie patch by hopping on turnip tops.

Hippety-hop! Hippety-hop! Hippety-hop!

a that

When Nihar thinks he is a master-chef, it is very funny.
As for dinner, he wants us all to have fries with honey!
Yuk! Yuk! Yuk!

a as for

When Milo is in the garden and a bumblebee buzzes in his ear, you will see Milo go crazy chasing his tail everywhere.

Ruff! Ruff! Ruff!

a you

When running in the hall I trip and fall.

I try and think of something funny and carry on as if nothing has happened at all.

Tsk! Tsk! Tsk!

We all are laughing. We all are a happy family.

Ha! Ha! Ha! Ha! Ha! Ha!

Starboard

Jobs to do

Play bingo!

Call out a word and let the child place her finger on the corresponding word.

you	for	a	that
as	of	you	for
that	a	of	as

Starboard

Talking point

1. What makes the children giggle?
2. What is mum trying to be?
3. What is hippety hopping?
4. Who thinks that he is a Master-Chef?
5. Would chips and honey be a tasty treat?
6. Why is Milo going 'ruff ruff'?
7. Ask the child the sounds some common animals make.
8. Explore what makes the child happy/ laugh.